NEWS FROM ME,
LUCY MCGEE

NEWS FROM ME, LUCY MCGEE

BY
MARY AMATO

ILLUSTRATED BY JESSICA MESERVE

Holiday House New York

HOLIDAY HOUSE is registered in the U.S. Patent and Trademark Office.
Printed and bound in July 2018 at Maple Press, York, PA, USA
First Edition
1 3 5 7 9 10 8 6 4 2
www.holidayhouse.com
Library of Congress Cataloging-in-Publication Data
Names: Amato, Mary, author.
Title: News from me, Lucy McGee / by Mary Amato.
Description: First edition. | New York : Holiday House, [2017]
Summary: Lucy avoids her school's new Uke Club to help neighbor
Scarlet create a Poetry Club, although Scarlet keeps telling
her to do things that seem wrong.
Identifiers: LCCN 2016058464 | ISBN 9780823438716 (hardcover)
Subjects: | CYAC: Behavior—Fiction. | Clubs—Fiction. | Honesty—Fiction.
Ukulele—Fiction.
Classification: LCC PZ7.A49165 New 2017 | DDC [Fic]—dc23 LC record
available at https://lccn.loc.gov/2016058464

For Busy Graham, Ukes on the Move,
and all those kids and uke-loving librarians
out there who light up when it's time to sing.

CONTENTS

Chapter One

NEWS FROM ME, LUCY MCGEE

Surprises are my favorite thing in the whole world unless it's a bad surprise. Bad surprises are things like no potato chips in your lunch. Good surprises are things like your dad calling up your mom at work and saying, "What the heck, let's get Lucy a puppy." That hasn't happened yet, but I keep hoping.

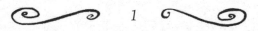

At recess today, I got a big surprise. Scarlett Tandy said she had a secret to tell me.

First she pulled me to the bottom of the hill so no one could hear. Then she said, "Lucy, I am going to have a new club. The Craft Club. Only girls who are invited can come. We're going to do fancy crafts and eat cookies and drink tea in real china cups."

I couldn't believe Scarlett Tandy was talking to me! Scarlett lives next to the school. She has a fat white cat named Princess Coconut and a sister, Brandy, in kindergarten and a pink bedroom with white carpeting that her sister can't play in. I don't know about the cat. She is rich. I don't think we're rich, because we don't have white carpeting and everybody can go in all the rooms.

"I love crafts!" I said. "I love cookies! I love tea!"

"You know the garden shed in my backyard?

My parents said I could have it. I'm going to turn it into a beautiful Craft Cottage with art supplies," she said. "That's where the club is going to meet."

"That sounds amazing," I said.

"I'm picking you to help me fix it up," she said. "Just you. Aren't you excited?" She started jumping up and down.

"I am! I am!" I started jumping up and down, too.

"We'll run to my house right after school," she said. "Yay! Yay! Yay!"

I stopped jumping. I had a problem. The new Songwriting Club at my school was having its first meeting today after school. My dad signed me up. He does things like that without asking me.

"Can we fix it up on another day?" I asked.

"No. I have lessons the other days," she said. "Say yes, Lucy!"

This was the opportunity of a lifetime.

When Scarlett and I were in first grade I had playdates at her house, and she let me look at her dolls and dollhouse, but I couldn't touch anything. I haven't been to her house since first grade. That's because Victoria and Mara and Resa got to be her best friends and also because Scarlett has violin and gymnastics. I am bad at lessons. I took violin and gymnastics at the same time as Scarlett and Victoria, and I couldn't do either, and I think that's why Scarlett stopped liking me.

"I'm supposed to go to the Songwriting Club," I said.

She made a face. "Phillip Lee's

4

club? My club is going to be way better. Just pretend you went to his club. Your parents will never know. This is going to be so much fun!"

Scarlett was inviting *me* to help her get the Craft Cottage ready. Not Victoria or Mara or Resa. Just me. Lucy McGee. I made up my mind. I was going to Scarlett's instead of the Songwriting Club. I was going to be sneaky.

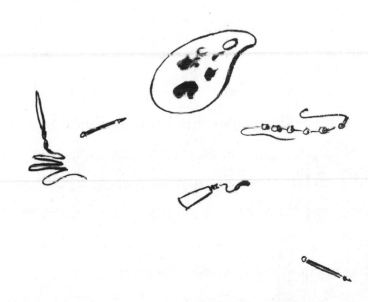

Chapter Two

OPEN YOUR EYES, HERE'S MY SURPRISE

"It's Wild Wednesday," Mr. Hopkin said. He's the art teacher at Slido Creek Elementary. Once a month in class we get to go wild and make whatever we want.

I decided to make a surprise present for Scarlett. All during art class, Mr. Hopkin let me work on the floor behind his desk so it could be a secret. Then he gave me a bag to put it in. I love Mr. Hopkin.

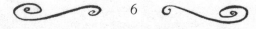

I was going to wait until Scarlett and I got to her house to give her the present, but I couldn't wait. As soon as school was over and we went outside, I took it out of my backpack.

"Ta-da," I said, and held it out.

Her face looked funny. "What is it?"

"It's a decoration for the Craft Cottage," I said. "I know you love white and pink and cats and crafts, so I put it all together." I handed her a sculpture of her cat, Princess Coconut. I made it out of white clay and pink pipe cleaners. I wanted to make it sparkly, but Mr. Hopkin didn't have white glitter, so I painted the whole cat with glue and sprinkled it with sugar that he had on his desk for his coffee. I also made a card with a poem in my fanciest writing.

I am a decoration.

I know I look delicious.

Don't eat me 'cause I'm made of

stuff that's not nutritious.

I cannot say meow

and I cannot purr.

I do not have a tail

and I do not have fur.

Don't pet me or my sugar

will come off and that's bad.

Then I will be naked

and you will be sad.

"It's very . . . um . . . creative, Lucy," she said.

"I can make you a pumpkin for Halloween and a turkey for Thanksgiving," I said.

"Well . . . the decorations for the Craft Cottage should be really pretty," she said. Then she called out to her sister, who was with the other kindergartners. "Hey, Brandy, we're going. Say good-bye to your little friends and get moving."

Brandy stuck her tongue out at Scarlett and ran ahead of us. Scarlett started chasing her, so I carried the Princess Coconut sculpture.

When we got to her house, Brandy went inside to watch TV, and Scarlett and I went through the gate to her backyard. The garden shed was smaller than I remembered. The brown walls were splattered with dirt, and the window was cracked. It looked like a sad, lumpy troll with one broken eye. But I didn't say anything because I didn't want to hurt her feelings.

"I got the supplies ready for us this morning," she said proudly.

She opened the door. There was a bucket, a sponge, a pair of yellow rubber gloves, a spray

bottle of cleaning stuff, and a pretty pink box. There was also a bunch of old garden tools.

"What's in the box?" I asked.

She set it outside on the patio table. "These are art supplies. One person is going to draw what the cottage should look like when it's done." She pulled out colored pencils and nice drawing paper.

"What's the other person going to do?" I asked.

"Clean the cottage," she said. "It'll be fun." She wrote "Craft Cottage" on the top of the drawing paper in fancy letters.

I peeked inside the shed. It was dark and smelled scary.

"I think whoever is best at art and at fancy writing should do the drawing part," she said. "Who do you think is better . . . me or you?" She drew the outline of the shed and quickly added some flowers around the edges.

"Well . . ." I put my sculpture on the patio table so she could see it sparkle. "We're both really good," I said. "But you—"

"Thanks!" She pointed to the rubber gloves and the bucket. "I'll draw. You can be like Snow White. You can whistle while you work."

I'm not good at whistling, so I just worked.

And worked.

And worked.

Just me. And a lot of dead bugs.

When Scarlett told me to throw out a bunch

of garbage, I saw my sculpture in the trash can. I blinked three times because I couldn't believe it.

Scarlett must have put it there by accident. I picked it up and put it on the floor in the cottage when she wasn't looking. And then I worked.

And worked.

And worked.

I was sweeping up the very last spiderweb when Scarlett came rushing in. "Lucy, put everything away," she said. "I heard my mom's car in the driveway. You have to go."

"I'm all done," I said. "Surprise!"

Scarlett looked at the cat sculpture in the corner and almost screamed. Ants were crawling all over it! That's what you call a bad surprise.

"Yuck. Get it out of here and go," Scarlett said.

I carried my Princess Coconut sculpture to the garbage can, and those ants didn't stop nibbling at it.

"Well, at least you guys like it," I whispered to the ants.

Working on the Craft Cottage was not as much fun as I thought. But Scarlett said that next Wednesday she'll have another surprise for me. I'm so excited I feel like I'm going to throw up!

Chapter Three

SING ALONG TO MY SONG

My baby sister, Lily, was getting eaten up by a crocodile when I got home. The crocodile was my brother, Leo. Leo is five and Lily is two. Leo was on his belly on the kitchen floor trying to chomp Lily's tiny feet. Lily was running around and screaming and saying "more," which is her favorite word.

My dad was making veggie burgers for dinner, and

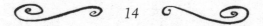

my mom wasn't home from work yet. "How was the Songwriting Club?" my dad asked.

My stomach started getting nervous. I should not have gone to Scarlett's without permission.

"The Songwriting Club was good," I said.

"Ms. Adamson said you'd write a new song each time," Dad said. "What song did you make up this time?"

"Um…we sang…" I had to think fast. "We sang a cleaning song."

"That sounds like a bad song," Leo said.

"Bad," Lily said.

"Hey, be a nice crocodile," Dad said to Leo. "You be nice, too, Lily. Sing it for us, Lucy."

Dad and Leo and Lily waited. I felt like there was a spotlight on me. I was nervous and then I

15

just started to sing about what happened after school.

Oh . . . I got a bucket
and a brand-new sponge
and I went to a dirty old shed.
I scrubbed the walls
and the ceiling and the floor
until my arms were dead.

Leo laughed. Lily laughed, too.

"Is that it?" Dad asked.

"No. There's more," I said, because it
seemed too short for a real song. So I sang:

There were beetles and bugs
and ants and slugs
and spiderwebs all droopy.

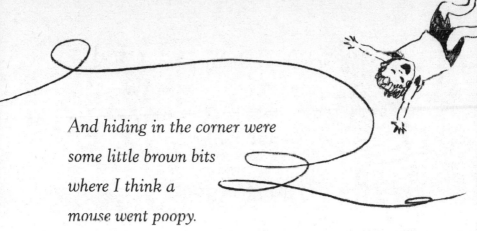

And hiding in the corner were some little brown bits where I think a mouse went poopy.

Leo and Lily fell down on the floor laughing.

"I have never heard a song quite like that!" My dad clapped.

Whew! They thought I went to the Songwriting Club, and they liked my song. Everything was great. Then it got even better because Leo turned back into a crocodile and started chomping all our toes, which was hilarious. *Ha-ha hee-hee!*

Chapter Four

FOR ME? WHAT WILL IT BE?

"What's my surprise?" I asked Scarlett every morning.

I was thinking it was cookies or fancy gel pens or maybe something really exciting for the Craft Cottage, like a pet. Sheep would be nice. We could give the sheep a haircut and then use the fluffy wool to knit crafts! I want a pet, but my parents say Leo acts like an animal so we don't need one.

"You have to wait until Wednesday after school for the surprise," Scarlett kept saying.

On Wednesday, as soon as school was over, I started jumping up and down. "What's my surprise, Scarlett?"

She pulled me over to the cubbies and smiled. "Today . . . drumroll, please . . . we are going to paint the inside of the cottage!" she whispered.

"That's it?" I asked.

"I thought you'd be excited, Lucy," she said.

I didn't want to hurt her feelings, so I said, "It's a great idea. I am excited. How about orange for the color? Orange is a happy color. It's my favorite."

"Orange is nice, but let's do pink," Scarlett whispered. "Mr. Hopkin said you could come to his room and get stuff. Get lots of pink paint and a cup to pour it in and a big paintbrush. Put it in this bag." She handed me a plastic bag.

"Me?" I asked.

"I have to meet Brandy and run home right away and get stuff ready. Come after you get the paint. Bye!" She left.

I went to the art room. The door was unlocked, but Mr. Hopkin wasn't there. I didn't know what to do. It felt funny to take paint without Mr. Hopkin being there, but Scarlett was waiting for me at her house. The clock on the wall went *tick, tick, tick*. My heart went *boom, boom, boom*.

I tiptoed over to the shelf and put two big bottles of pink paint, a cup, and two paintbrushes in my bag. The bad feeling in my stomach got worse. I tiptoed out.

Luckily no one was in the hallway. I started to run, and when I turned the corner . . . *Bam!* I bumped right into Phillip Lee. Phillip is in my class. He is the one who started the Songwriting Club. I screamed and dropped my bag, and he dropped his ukulele. Oh no! We both threw out our arms. I caught his uke. He dove for my bag.

"Sorry!" I yelped, and handed him back his uke.

"I was looking for you," he said, and handed me the bag. "Ms. Adamson said you're signed up for my Songwriting Club. She sent me to find you."

"My dad signed me up," I explained. "But I can't be in the club. I'm working on . . . a project. Bye."

I started to leave. Seeing Phillip made me remember that I should have told my parents that I was going to Scarlett's instead of the Songwriting Club. I was breaking the rule again.

"The Songwriting Club is fun," he said. "We're making up songs and learning how to play them on the uke. Ms. Adamson has ukes to borrow."

I kept walking.

He called out: "A uke only has four strings, so it's easier to play than a guitar."

I thought about that while I ran to Scarlett's house. Maybe if it was easy, even I could learn to play it. But I stopped thinking about it when I got to Scarlett's house because she cheered when she saw the bag full of paint.

"Yay, Lucy! This is going to be so much fun!"

I hoped so. I needed some fun. I also needed a cookie. Throw in some potato chips and I'd have the best day ever!

Chapter Five

THINK PINK

"I'll let you paint the walls," Scarlett said when we got to her backyard. "That's the best part."

"I got two brushes," I said. "We could do it together."

"I have to paint a sign in fancy letters that says 'Private' so Brandy and her little twerpy friends don't come in."

She had a point.

I went into the shed and got started while she sat on the patio and painted her sign. I think my job might have been harder, because she got hers done before I did and went inside. I heard the TV coming from her family room, but I didn't think she would watch TV while I was working. She was probably getting snacks for us.

After I finished the first wall, I dipped my paintbrush into the paint and brought it over to the next wall. It dripped on my cheek and dropped on my nose. It glipped on my knees and glopped on my toes. When you paint, this fact is true: Paint will get all over you!

Hey, that would make a great song, I thought to myself.

It drips on your cheek and drops on your nose.
It glips on your knees and glops on your toes.
When you paint, this fact is true:
Paint will get all over you!

I was painting the last wall when I heard a sound. Scarlett was coming. I ran to the door just as a white fur ball darted into the Craft Cottage. It wasn't Scarlett. It was Scarlett's cat, Princess Coconut, and my foot was about to land on her head. She leaped to the left and I leaped to the right. The good surprise was that my foot didn't hit her. The bad surprise was that my foot hit the cup of paint.

SPLATTER! SPLAM!

Uh-oh.

Princess Coconut wasn't white anymore. She looked like a giant pink gumball that somebody slobbered on.

Scarlett walked in. "Are you done, Lu—" She looked at the cat.

"She looks pretty in pink," I said. "Don't you think?" Then I said, "Hey, that rhymes!" I was on a roll with the rhymes.

"Who cares about rhymes?" Scarlett screamed. "You need to wash Princess Coconut or we're in big trouble."

Just then, the cat darted out of the cottage.

We both ran after her. Scarlett caught the cat and I grabbed the garden hose. I turned it on and aimed it at the cat. Scarlett screamed, "*Stop!*"

It took me a few seconds to

27

figure out how to turn it off. Both Scarlett and the cat were dripping wet. Princess Coconut hissed at me, jumped out of Scarlett's arms, and ran into the house.

"Well, she isn't pink anymore," I said.

"Thanks a lot," Scarlett said.

I gave her my hoodie to dry off.

She grabbed her sign off the table. Water had gotten all over it. "Oh no! I worked hard on this," she cried. "It had no drips. Now it's a mess."

"Sorry. But at least I finished painting," I said to cheer her up. "Check it out."

We went into the Craft Cottage and looked at the walls.

"Oh no!" she screamed. "This is bad, too, Lucy. It's drippy. And it's not very pink."

She was right. It was drippy and it didn't look pink.

"Real life is not turning out the way I want," she said sadly. "In my head, this whole thing was really pretty."

I know how that feels. I tried to make a lion costume for Halloween out of yellow pajamas and brown face paint, and I just looked like an old banana with bruises.

"Don't worry, Scarlett," I said. "We can still make the cottage look pretty. I'll bring something special."

She looked up, and her eyes were watery like she was going to cry. "Not another cat sculpture," she said.

"Something really pretty," I said.

"Okay, Lucy. Thanks." She gave me a little hug. I'm sure she would have given me a big hug, but I had paint on me.

Chapter Six

A BUBBLE AND SOME TROUBLE

Think. Think. Think. What could I bring to cheer up Scarlett?

I looked all over the house. In the dining room cupboard I found my mom's pretty teapot with the tiny pink flowers. As Leo would say, Scarlett would go peepee in her pants over that. I didn't think my parents would mind if I borrowed it for a little while, so I hid it in my backpack.

The next morning, I gave it to Scarlett. She jumped up and down.

"Lucy! I love it!" she said, and gave me a big hug.

A huge bubble of happiness filled me up on the inside, big enough to last for the rest of my life.

Then something terrible happened, and the bubble of happiness went *poof!*

The Morning Mix TV show started. The fifth graders get to do school announcements every morning on their TV show, and we all watch it. Devon, the fifth grader who was hosting the show, said that Mr. Hopkin had a special announcement.

Mr. Hopkin came on the TV. Mr. Hopkin smiles a lot, but today he had a frown. "I am sad to say that two bottles of pink paint and two paintbrushes are missing from the art room," he said. He was looking into the camera, but I felt like he was looking right at me. "We have never had a problem with stealing here at Slido Creek Elementary, and I hope this is a mistake rather than a crime. If any of you know anything about this, please come and talk to me."

I remembered that Phillip Lee saw me with the bag of paint. He would tell Mr. Hopkin about me! I was too afraid to look at him. I looked at Scarlett, but she was very busy with her shoelace and she wouldn't look up.

All morning, I thought the police would come and take me away. I had to wait until recess to talk to Scarlett.

Finally recess came and Scarlett and I ran down to the fence where nobody could hear us.

Her face was red.

"Don't tell anyone or you'll get in trouble, Lucy," she said.

"But you told me that Mr. Hopkin said I could take the paint," I said.

She shook her head. "I said he *probably* would let you take it if you asked nicely."

"You did not, Scarlett! I would remember that."

"You don't have a good memory, Lucy," she said. "You're mad at me because you stole the paint without asking."

"I didn't steal it! You told me it was okay. It was your idea, Scarlett."

"It was my idea to ask, not to steal, Lucy."

Maybe Scarlett was right. Maybe I didn't have a good memory. This was terrible. The whole thing was making my stomach hurt. "I'm going to tell Mr. Hopkin the truth," I said, and started to leave.

She grabbed my arm. "Lucy," she said, "if you say anything about me or the paint, I will get in trouble, and I will never be your friend and nobody will want to be your friend because they'll find out that you ruined everything."

My stomach hurt more. I walked away.

"What are you going to do?" she asked.

"I'm going to stick my head in a garbage can. That's my big exciting plan," I said.

Another rhyme. And I wasn't even trying.

I walked up to the black-
top and sat by myself. I felt like somebody was watching me. Mr. Hopkin had
probably hired a detective who was hiding
in the bushes with binoculars. I was probably going to get arrested and go to jail. While
Scarlett and Victoria and Mara and Resa got to
make crafts and have cookies and tea in the Craft
Cottage, I'd be in jail with beetles and bugs and
centipedes and slugs and droopy spiderwebs and
poopy mice and real robbers who were probably smelly and mean. All the teachers would be
in the teachers' lounge saying, "What a shame
about Lucy McGee. She used to be a nice girl."
And my mom and dad would cry. And
Leo and Lily would miss me.

I could not let that happen. I had
to fix this. Think. Think. Think.

And then it hit me. I ran over and pulled Scarlett away from Victoria and Mara. "We can buy pink paint and return it to Mr. Hopkin's room without anybody finding out," I said. "If the paint is returned, we can't get in trouble."

She clapped. "That's the best idea you've ever had," she said, and smiled. "On Monday, I don't have my violin lesson because my violin teacher is having a roof canal. So I'll get my babysitter to take us to the art store after school."

"Yay!" I said.

"But only if you promise not to tell anybody anything," she said.

"I promise," I said. "We have a plan that will not fail, and I won't have to go to jail!"

Another rhyme!

Hmmm . . . maybe I should be a songwriter.

Chapter Seven

FUNNY MONEY

Eleven bucks. That's how much we needed for our secret plan. Paint costs a lot.

I couldn't tell my parents what it was for, so I just said I wanted to buy some special art supplies. My dad said that I could earn money on Saturday by cleaning the basement. More sponges. More spiders. Yippee. Scarlett promised to come over after gymnastics and help.

On Saturday, I scrubbed and mopped and dusted. Scarlett didn't come.

I called her on the phone, and her dad said she went over to Victoria's after gymnastics. Her memory wasn't that good after all.

I didn't whistle while I worked, but I sang, and that made it fun. I like to sing, and I got eleven dollars!

On Monday, I brought the money to school in my pocket. When I walked down the hall, it felt funny to have eleven dollars in my pocket. *I hope I do not get robbed*, I thought. I would be so sad. Then I thought about how sad Mr. Hopkin was to find out his paint was stolen.

All day, I felt like there were eyes on me.

After school, Scarlett's babysitter took us to the art store and we bought the paint. "It's for school," Scarlett told the babysitter, which was true. "We need to bring it back right away."

She let us go back to school. It was four o'clock. The teachers were all having a meeting in the cafeteria. The hallways were quiet.

"You put the stuff back in the art room," Scarlett said. "I'll wait by the cafeteria. If anybody comes out, I'll talk so they won't follow you."

"Why don't you put the stuff back?" I asked.

"You have quieter shoes than me," she said. It was true. She had on fancy shoes with little heels that went *click, click, click, click.*

I tiptoed down the hall to the art room with the bag of paint. My heart was beating fast. The door to the art room was closed. I turned the knob and peeked in. It was dark. Mr. Hopkin was nowhere in sight. I crept in and headed toward the paint shelf.

"Robber!" someone yelled, and flipped on the lights.

Chapter Eight

UNSTEAL, FOR REAL

I jumped and turned around.

Phillip Lee was standing there with a bag of potato chips. "I knew you were the robber!" Phillip Lee said. "I knew you'd strike again!" He jumped up and down with glee, and some potato chips went flying.

"Shh! I'm not stealing, Phillip! I'm actually doing the

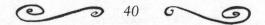

opposite of stealing. I'm unstealing." I showed him the pink paint. "See, I'm putting it back."

He stopped jumping. "What?"

"I'm not a real robber. I took the paint by accident. I thought I had permission. I'm returning it."

"Oh," he said. "I've been spying on you. It looked like you were plotting with Scarlett. I thought you were planning on stealing more."

"Did you tell Mr. Hopkin that you saw me with the paint?"

"No," he said. "I wanted to surprise him by catching you in the act."

I put the paint and the brushes and the cup back. "Please don't say anything to anybody about this, Phillip. I don't want to get in trouble. And I don't want Scarlett to get in trouble."

He looked like he wasn't sure what to do.

"Does Mr. Hopkin know you're in here?" I asked.

"No," he said. "I snuck in so I could catch you."

"I don't think students are supposed to be in teachers' rooms after school even if they are trying to catch robbers," I said. "So let's both drop it." I started to walk out.

"Wait. What did you want the paint for?" he asked.

"It's a secret," I said.

"What kind of a secret?"

"A secret club kind of secret."

"Why don't you just come to Songwriting Club?" he asked. "It's fun." He set down his potato chips and picked up his uke, which was on one of the art tables. "I wrote a song while I was waiting to catch you."

He played and sang:

I know who likes to steal.
I'm quite a good detective.
All day I hide and spy.
I'm really quite effective.
So if you want to rob a school,
a store, a house, or bank,
I'll catch you in the act
And everyone will thank . . .
Me, me, me!
I catch robbers as they flee.
Me, me, me!
I catch robbers named
McGee.

He held out his uke. "You
can try it."

I took it in my
hands. I didn't know
what I was doing, but
I pretended to strum as
I sang:

> I really like your song,
> except for the last line.
> Because Lucy McGee
> would never do a crime.
> So please stop catching robbers
> as they try to flee
> and stick to playing songs
> on your ukulele.

Phillip smiled. "You really should join the club."

He held out his bag of potato chips. "Want one?"

That made me smile for two reasons. Nothing like a compliment and a potato chip! Yum! Yum!

I ran outside and told Scarlett the news. "The paint is back," I said. "Everything is okeydokey."

She gave me a big hug. "We can decorate on Wednesday. It'll be so much fun. I told Victoria, Mara, and Resa that the cottage would be ready for our first club meeting the Wednesday after that. They can't wait!"

Chapter Nine

WHY CAN'T THERE BE TWO OF ME?

Sometimes things get stuck in my brain and they don't want to come out. I kept thinking about the fun song Phillip made up and what a happy sound his ukulele made when he was strumming it. I also liked the way he smiled when I made up my song on the spot. I wanted to go to the Songwriting Club. I also wanted to help with the Craft Club. I wish I had two of me so I could do two things at once.

On Wednesday, I met Scarlett at the flagpole after school. I had an idea.

"Maybe we should go to the Songwriting Club first and then go to the Craft Club," I said. "In the Songwriting Club, we could make up songs. And then we could sing them in the Craft Club."

She made a face. "Boys don't know how to have a good club."

I didn't think that was true. Leo made up a very good club last summer called the Sharks in the Park Club where everybody in our family went to the park and pretended to be sharks. How can that not be a good club? Before I could say anything, Scarlett pulled me along.

While Brandy and the babysitter watched TV, Scarlett and I moved stools and a table into the shed. We put a tablecloth and a vase with flowers from the garden on the table, and it really did look pretty. And then the door opened and a man's face poked in and we screamed.

It was Scarlett's dad, home from work early.

He didn't have a happy look on his face at all. Brandy popped her head in, too.

"What are you girls doing?" he asked.

"We're decorating," Scarlett said.

"Did you ask your mom?" he asked.

"She didn't," Brandy said. "I told her she was going to be in trouble."

Scarlett made a face at Brandy. Then she turned back to her dad. "Lucy wanted to have a club in here."

"Me?" I looked at Scarlett, but she wouldn't look back.

"What did you do with my gardening tools?" her dad asked.

My stomach knotted up.

"I didn't touch them," Scarlett said.

"Lucy?" Her dad looked at me.

"I put them in the garbage can," I said.

"You what?" he yelled. "Those were good tools!"

"Uh-oh. You're in big trouble, Lucy," Brandy said.

"That's where Scarlett told me to put them," I said.

"I said put them in the garage, not in the garbage!" Scarlett yelled.

"No you didn't!" I yelled. "Stop lying!"

Her dad stepped between us. "You both should have known that you needed permission before you did anything out here." He looked around. "Who painted the walls? It looks terrible."

"Lucy did," Scarlett said.

"Scarlett told me we could do whatever we wanted," I said.

Scarlett made a sad face and looked at her dad. "I'm sorry, Daddy. Lucy seemed so happy about the idea, I didn't want to disappoint her."

Her dad pulled out his phone and called somebody. At first I thought it was the police, and then I heard him say my dad's name. "Moz, this is Roger. I'm sending Lucy home. She talked Scarlett into turning our shed into a clubhouse and basically made a mess of everything. She threw out my perfectly good gardening tools and slapped some kind of kiddie paint all over the walls."

I couldn't hear my dad's voice. He was probably having a heart attack.

Scarlett started crying, but it didn't look like real crying to me.

"Ha-ha, told you so," Brandy said.

"Go inside, Scarlett," her dad said. "You, too, Brandy. Lucy, your dad said you should walk home."

Scarlett and Brandy went inside. Before the back door closed, Princess Coconut came out and hissed at me.

That cat didn't like me. I didn't care. I didn't like her, either. *From now on*, I thought, *I'm calling her Princess Dodobutt.*

Chapter Ten

WHO WANTS A SAD DAD?

If you know you'll be in trouble when you go home, you don't exactly want to run there. I walked as slowly as I possibly could. First I took slow, small steps. Then I went zigzag. But my stomach was hurting, so I finally went straight.

My dad was sitting on the front steps, waiting for me. Leo and Lily were in the yard playing Pig on a Blanket.

Pig on a Blanket is when you get a blanket and you pretend to be a pig on it. Seeing Leo and Lily oinking and wiggling their pretend tails made me feel sadder. When I was Leo's age, I was cute and got to play games. Now that I am nine, life is one big problem after another.

"What did you do at Scarlett's, Lucy?" my dad asked. His face looked like a rainy day.

The truth gushed out. I told my dad that I put Mr. Tandy's tools in the garbage can. I told him that I took the paint from Mr. Hopkin's room. I told him that I didn't go to the Songwriting Club. I even told him that I borrowed Mom's teapot. I started to cry, and it was real crying because all those things in one list made me realize how bad I had been.

He hugged me and said, "Lucy, it's hard sometimes to know what's right and wrong.

But if you have a feeling in your gut that something isn't right, you have to listen to that feeling instead of listening to someone like Scarlett."

"I know," I said. "My gut said that I shouldn't have gone to Scarlett's without permission. My gut said that I shouldn't have put tools in the garbage can. My gut said that I shouldn't have taken the paint or the teapot. My gut said a lot!"

"Then why didn't you stand up to Scarlett?" he asked.

"She's very tall," I said.

My dad laughed for some reason. His rainy-day face went away, so I hugged him, and he hugged me back.

"If someone else talks you into doing something wrong, you still have to apologize for what you did. Write a letter to Scarlett's parents. And you're going to have to replace their tools."

"I don't have any more money."

He gave me a look.

"Oh no! More cleaning?" I asked.

He nodded. "Yep. Garage."

"I think Scarlett should apologize to me for lying," I said.

"I agree," my dad said. "But you can't make somebody else apologize."

"*You* can," I said.

He smiled. "I'm only the boss of *this* family."

Leo and Lily ran over and we had a Big Pig Hug. A Big Pig Hug is a big hug with pigs. *Oink. Oink.*

Even though my dad makes me do things I don't want to do, I'm glad I'm in this family.

I wrote my letter right away, and my stomach started feeling better.

Dear Mr. and Mrs. Tandy,

I'm sorry that I threw away the tools and that I painted the walls of the shed without permission. I have learned that if Scarlett says it's okay to do something, I should get proof.

You did not mention the cat, but I accidentally got paint on her. I'm sorry. I want to apologize for everything so you know I am an honest person.

I am doing extra chores to make money so I can buy you new gardening tools. If I ever get invited to your house again, I will never put anything in the garbage. Except garbage. But only if I'm sure it's garbage.

Sincerely,

Lucy McGee

P.S. I need the teapot back.

In fact, my stomach felt so
much better, I played with Leo and Lily.
What did we play? Pig on a Blanket, of course.
Oink. Oink.

Chapter Eleven

BIG LITTLE PIGS

I wrote a new song.
Maybe I should join
the Songwriting Club!

PIGGY SONG

by Lucy McGee

We are the Piggies.

We love our cuddly blanket.
We play so much upon it
we actually should thank it.

Wrap a little piggy
in a blanky . . . so snug!
Come on, little Piggies,
have a Big Pig Hug.

We wag our tails,
and we wiggle them some more.
We say, "Oink oink."
Then we sleep and snore.

Wrap a little piggy
in a blanky . . . so snug!
Come on, little Piggies,
have a Big Pig Hug.

Chapter Twelve

HAPPY FEET? NOT ME

On Monday morning, Phillip Lee gave me a note. His handwriting isn't fancy like Scarlett's, but it's happy handwriting.

> This Wednesday after school
> come and play the uke.
> It's really fun to sing and strum.
> It won't make you puke.

After I read it, Scarlett grabbed the note. She read it and laughed. "Go ahead, Lucy. That's the perfect club for you." She made a mean face.

"Perhaps you should start a new club, Scarlett," I said. "It can be called the Mean Face Club."

"Ha-ha-ha," she said.

That night, I told my parents I was going to the Songwriting Club for sure. They were excited. I was excited.

By Wednesday, my brain started getting nervous. My stomach, too. I was afraid that I wouldn't be good at making up songs in front of other people. And I was afraid I wouldn't be good at the ukulele. Phillip and the other kids would find out I had no talent and kick me out. I couldn't play the violin or do gymnastics. I couldn't even clean or paint right. Why did I think I could ever do something like sing and play the ukulele? After school, I told my feet to walk to the music room, but instead they started walking to the school doors. Phillip Lee stopped me with his uke in his hand.

"It's Wednesday, Lucy."

"I know. I . . . I have to go home."

"What about the Songwriting Club?"

"I have a sore throat," I said. Now that I thought about it, my throat did feel scratchy.

Phillip looked sad. "If you feel better, come next week," he said.

He went to the music room, and I started walking out.

I tiptoed back. The music room door was open a crack. I peeked in.

There was a circle of chairs, but only Ms. Adamson and Phillip were there. Ms. Adamson

had a green uke and Phillip had his blue uke. There were other ukes waiting on the empty chairs. Purple. Pink. Even orange. The color of happy.

"Teach me how to play your new song," Ms. Adamson said.

Phillip showed her how to press down a string with her left hand and strum with her right hand.

"I keep making mistakes," Ms. Adamson said.

"You're just learning," Phillip said. "Everybody is bad when they're just learning. I was, too. I'll play it once and then we'll do it together. Really slowly."

They started strumming. Ms. Adamson is really nice. She made Phillip smile, but I think Phillip still looked kind of sad and lonely because teachers don't really count as people when you have a club.

I wanted to go in, but my feet wouldn't listen. All the way home, I sang to my feet.

Feet, feet. Listen to me.
Next week, it's the ukulele.

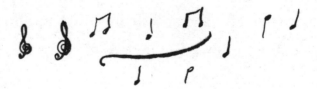

Chapter Thirteen

SHOULD I GO?
YES OR NO?

Dear Phillip,

Here is a letter

to say my throat is better.

I'm coming on Wednesday.

Um...

(I just tried to think of something that rhymes with

Wednesday and I got stuck.)

—Lucy

I had told my parents about chickening out, and they said I should give it another try. So on Monday I gave Phillip the note.

He passed me a note back with a big smile.

Dear Lucy,
Wednesday is hard to rhyme.
I just tried to do it seven times.
—Phillip

The Songwriting Club was going to be fun. I was going to be brave and just do it.

But then on Tuesday when I got to school, everything got jumbly again.

Scarlett ran over to me. "Lucy! Guess what! My parents decided it was a good idea to turn the shed into a Craft Cottage. Last night, my mom helped me decorate it. We got another teapot and lots of fancy supplies like 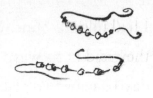 beads and glitter and yarn. Isn't that great?"

"Um . . . that's amazing," I said.

"Tomorrow is going to be the first club meeting. I'm going to tell Mara, Victoria, and Resa," she said. "You have to come."

"What about having it on Saturday?" I whispered.

"No. It's tomorrow. Brandy is playing at a friend's house, so she won't bother us. My mom is going to come home from work early and make cookies and real tea with clotted cream." She started jumping up and down again and hugging me at the same time, so I had to jump up and down, too. Then the other girls walked in and Scarlett ran to invite them.

I looked around to see if Phillip had heard Scarlett, but he wasn't in the room. Now I really wanted to be two places at the same time. I didn't know what I was going to do.

Our teacher called for everyone to sit down for *The Morning Mix*.

I was wondering where Phillip was when he came on the TV. He was a surprise guest on *The Morning Mix*.

"Hi! My name is Phillip Lee. I'm here to tell you about the Songwriting Club."

Phillip strummed his blue ukulele. "We make up songs and play them. You can come tomorrow. You don't need an instrument. Ms. Adamson has ukes and you can check one out like a library book."

Everyone in our class stared at the screen.

Nobody from our class had ever been on *The Morning Mix*.

"If Phillip gets to be on *The Morning Mix*," Scarlett said, "other clubs should get to be on."

Saki, the fifth grader who was on TV, said, "That's great, Phillip. How many people are in the Songwriting Club?"

"Well," Phillip said, "right now it's only me."

Scarlett laughed in a mean way. "You can't have a club with only one person." Victoria and Mara and some boys started laughing, too.

On the screen Phillip said, "But Lucy McGee is coming tomorrow!"

Everybody looked at me and started laughing.

"I'm not really joining," I said quickly. "I just said that to make Phillip feel better."

On TV, Phillip turned to Saki. "If we practice a song, maybe we can play it on *The Morning Mix*."

"Great idea." Saki looked at the camera. "You heard it here on *The Morning Mix*. Now it's time for the weather."

Everybody in our class started talking.

"I'm going to get our club on TV," Scarlett said to Victoria. "We can show off the crafts we make."

Mrs. Brock, our teacher, looked up from her desk. "Too much chitchatting."

When *The Morning Mix* was over and Phillip came back to our room, Mrs. Brock said, "Phillip, we saw you on TV."

"*The Morning Mix* is not real TV," Scarlett said. "My mom is on real TV."

Scarlett's mom does the weather on Channel 4.

"Let's all have a round of applause for Phillip," Mrs. Brock said, and she made everybody in the room clap. That was not smart because when you make people clap, it doesn't sound real. I'm sorry to say this because I like Mrs. Brock, but sometimes even good teachers make mistakes.

I felt terrible for Phillip.

Later that day, Scarlett walked by and dropped a note in my lap.

Dear Lucy,

You have to be careful who you're friends with. Friends will make your whole life either good or bad. If you're friends with Phillip nobody will like you. I am not saying this to be mean to Phillip. I'm saying it because I want to be nice to you. Just so you know. You have a choice. You can either go to the Songwriting Club or you can come to my Craft Club.

Love, Scarlett

Even though I was mad at Scarlett for being mean to Phillip, I didn't want the other girls to laugh at me and I didn't want to miss out on the Craft Club.

I wrote back in my fanciest handwriting.

Dear Scarlett,

Phillip didn't hear me right. I am coming to the Craft Club, not the Songwriting Club. I am excited to do crafts and have cookies and tea with you, Victoria, Mara, and Resa. I don't know what clotted cream is, but the cream part sounds fancy even if the clotted part doesn't sound so good.

Your best friend,

Lucy

Okay. I was back to going to Scarlett's instead of the Songwriting Club, which meant I had to tell my parents . . . and Phillip.

Chapter Fourteen

OH DEAR, THE BIG DAY IS HERE!

You know how it is when you're supposed to do something but you don't want to do it? It happens to Leo all the time, and he always does the same thing. He turns into an animal. Last night at dinner, he was supposed to finish his rice and beans before he got dessert, and he turned into a turtle and tucked his head inside his shirt and wouldn't come out.

I didn't want to tell my parents about Scarlett's club because I knew that they would tell me to stick with the Songwriting Club. They didn't understand how important the Craft Club was. All night I tried to think of a way to tell them. Then at breakfast I got a great idea. I would pretend to go to the Songwriting Club one more time. At the Craft Club, I would make an amazing present for my parents and give it to them. They would love it and want me to stay in the club. Who doesn't love presents?

After school, Scarlett, Victoria, Mara, Resa, and I met outside. It was so exciting to be part of the group.

"Lucy and I are going to go first to get everything set up," Scarlett told the other girls. "So wait here for five minutes and then come."

I couldn't believe it. She picked me! I bet Victoria, Mara, and Resa all wished that they could be the one to help her set up.

When Scarlett and I got to her house, the babysitter was saying good-bye to someone on the phone.

"That was your mom," the babysitter told Scarlett. "She couldn't get out of work. She said to have fun."

Scarlett started to cry. "But she was going to make cookies and tea and clotted cream."

"I'm sure we have some cookies in the pantry," the babysitter said.

"The cookies we have aren't even pretty," Scarlett said. "They should at least have frosting on them."

I felt sad for Scarlett.

"We can make the whole thing look pretty," I said.

I found some strawberries in the refrigerator and put the strawberries and cookies on a plate in a fancy way. We made iced tea and put it in a pitcher. The babysitter helped us put the tea and cookies on a tray. "See?" I said. "It's beautiful."

"You're right, Lucy," Scarlett said, and smiled. It was like the sun coming out again, which made me feel happy.

Out the window we could see Victoria, Mara, and Resa walk into the backyard. "It's time!" Scarlett said, and handed me the tray. "Wait! I have something special for you!" She tied a fancy lace apron around me. "There! Isn't that pretty?"

"What about you?" I asked. "Don't you have one?"

"You get to wear it," she said.

"What about cups and plates?" I asked.

"The cups and plates are already out there," she said. "Come on!"

She ran out to the backyard and I followed, but I didn't run because I didn't want to spill.

"Welcome to the Craft Club," Scarlett said. "As you can see, we will be sipping iced tea and making beautiful things in this elegant Craft Cottage."

"Wow," Victoria said.

"This is so exciting," Mara said.

Resa looked at the cookies on my tray and said, "Yum!"

"I have wonderful refreshments," Scarlett said. "Do come inside, won't you?"

Scarlett opened the door and we walked in.

There were four cups, four plates, and four chairs. Victoria, Mara, Resa, and Scarlett all sat down.

"While we are being served our tea and cookies, I will show you the exciting craft we'll be making today," Scarlett said.

The table was too small and full to set the tray on. I just stood there, not knowing what to do.

Scarlett set a tray of beads on the table, and the girls *oohed*. "We're going to make our own necklaces on these pretty satin cords!" She handed Victoria, Mara, and Resa each a cord and set one out for herself. Then she snapped her fingers at me. "Lucy, we need our refreshments. My guests are absolutely starved."

My face turned redder than the straw-berries. She didn't pick me to help her because she wanted me to be her best friend. She picked me to help her because she wanted me to be her maid.

I wanted to cry. Or scream. But then I thought . . . maybe if the other girls believed I wanted to be the maid, it wouldn't be as embarrassing.

I let go of the tray with my right hand to serve the cookies. But when I took the plate of cookies off, the tray tilted and the pitcher started to slide!

Chapter Fifteen

A CHILLING SPILLING

I let go of the cookie plate and grabbed the pitcher before it crashed on Resa's head. That was the good news. The bad news was that the lid popped off and the iced tea gushed out. It poured on Resa's beautiful hair and dripped down her face.

"Lucy!" Scarlett screamed.

The girls all looked at Resa.

Resa got up and squeezed the iced tea out of her hair. "I hear tea makes an excellent shampoo," she said, and laughed.

I tried to help, but Scarlett yelled at me. "Don't move, Lucy! You'll make things worse!"

"I think I should go home and take a real shower," Resa said. "See you guys at school tomorrow. The cottage is really cool, Scarlett. Thanks."

"I'm sorry, Resa," I said.

"It's okay, Lucy," she said.

After she left, Scarlett turned to me. "It's not okay. You've spoiled everything!"

I tried to pick up the cookies, and she snapped, "Go inside and make more tea."

By the time I came out with the tea, the girls were putting on their necklaces. Victoria had made an extra one for Resa. They didn't make one for me.

I didn't know what to do, so I just stood there.

"This is the *best* club," Victoria said.

"I simply can't wait for next Wednesday already!" Mara said. "It's much better than anything at school."

"Yes. It's much better than Phillip Lee's Songwriting Club," Victoria said, and Scarlett laughed.

"Anything is better than Phillip Lee's club," Scarlett said.

Victoria and Mara laughed.

For the first time in my life, I wanted to be a bug. If I were a bug I wouldn't have to stand there and hold the iced tea and listen to them say mean things. I could crawl away and nobody would notice.

Chapter Sixteen

FROWNS AND
LETDOWNS

When I got to my house, two cars were in the driveway. Ms. Adamson and Phillip's mom were in the doorway talking to my dad! Phillip was sitting on the steps by the driveway.

"Lucy!" my dad yelled when he saw me. "Thank God you're all right!"

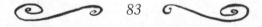

Everybody turned to look at me.

"Phillip said you were coming to the Songwriting Club for sure," Ms. Adamson said. "When you didn't show up, we all got worried."

"Where were you?" my dad asked.

I didn't know what to say. "Um . . ."

"Were you at Scarlett's again?" Dad asked.

I could tell that Phillip was looking at me, but I couldn't look back.

"Come on, Mom," Phillip said.

"I'm glad you're home safe and sound, Lucy," his mom said and they left.

"I'm sorry," I said.

Ms. Adamson left, too.

"Lucy, I am disappointed," my dad said. "You're telling lies. You know the rule. We have to know where you are. We thought you might have been hurt or even kidnapped. You let down

Phillip, too, by promising to come and then not showing. Go to your room and think about this. You and Mom and I need to have a big talk tonight."

I ran past my dad and all the way up the stairs to my room. I slammed my bedroom door, and I slammed my closet door. *Slam. Slam.*

When I'm very upset, I sit on the floor in my closet. I usually keep the door open because I don't like the dark. And I usually sit on the special pillow that I keep in there that I call my ice-cream pillow because it is soft and white. But this time I threw the pillow out of the closet and sat on the cold hard floor and closed the door tight. That just shows you how upset I was.

After a while, I heard some little feet and then the door opened and there was a wolf looking at me. It wasn't a real wolf. It was Leo with his wolf mask on. Actually, the mask doesn't really look like a wolf face, it's just a paper plate with a lot of brown crayon marks on it, but we know it's a wolf.

Leo lifted the mask. "Mom's home."

I didn't say anything.

"Are you mad or sad?" he asked.

"I'm mad and sad."

"That's bad," Leo said.

Mad. Sad. Bad. Those were some good

rhymes. I could make a song out of that, I thought, and then I remembered that I wasn't in the Songwriting Club or the Craft Club, and I wanted to cry.

"Go like this," Leo said, and he leaned his head back and howled like a wolf.

"*Aawooo!*" Well, he's only five, so it was more like a baby wolf.

"Why should I do that?" I asked.

"It's what us wolves do when we're mad or sad, and it makes us feel better. Do it."

I yelled, "You're not a wolf, Leo! You're a human being! Go away!" I slammed the door again.

He started crying.

Let me tell you something. Hearing a little wolf cry outside your door makes you want to stay in a dark closet forever.

"Cry in your own room," I said. I heard him run. Lily's little footsteps followed.

I felt terrible. I thought about all the cleaning I did for Scarlett and all the creepy bugs I swept up or flicked away. Most of them were dead, but that's the thing about bugs. Even the dead ones are creepy. I thought about how she tricked me into being her maid. All because of Scarlett, I had ruined my chances of being in the Songwriting Club, lied to my parents, and yelled at poor Leo. Twice.

I got madder and madder and then I howled. "*Aawoo!*"

Leo was right. It felt good to howl.

"*Aawoo!*"

In the distance I heard a sound coming from Leo and Lily's room.

"*Aawoo!*"

I crawled out of my closet.

"*Aawoo!*"

Leo was sitting in his closet howling, and Lily was standing there sucking on her pacifier looking at him.

"I'm sorry I yelled at you, Leo. You're right about howling."

"Go away," he said.

Lily took her pacifier out and pointed it at me. "Bad."

And then they both howled.

Chapter Seventeen

MAKE-IT-BETTER LETTERS

Get ready, fingers. After the long talk with my mom and dad, I had a lot of writing to do.

Dear Ms. Adamson,

I'm sorry I made you worry. I know you have better things to do after school than to drive to my house and see me get in trouble. Unfortunately, I have been on a roll with being bad, but I'm really trying to improve. My mom said I scared the living daylights out of you. I don't know what that is, but I hope this letter puts the living daylights back in.

Sincerely,

Lucy McGee

Dear Phillip's Mom,

I know that you took time out of your busy day to help find me. That was a total waste of your time because I wasn't lost or kidnapped or anything. I'm sorry. I also know that grown-ups have lives for Pete's sake. My dad said that. I'm not sure who Pete is, but I know it's important. Thank you and it won't happen again.

Sincerely,

Lucy McGee

Dear Phillip,

I promised you I would go to your club and then I did a take-back without even telling you. I'm sorry. I kind of did it twice, because that day I said my throat hurt it didn't really. You were excellent on *THE MORNING MIX*.

Lucy

Chapter Eighteen

SNEAKY ME

On Monday, I gave everybody my "sorry" letters. Phillip still wouldn't look at me.

During math, I kept thinking about Scarlett and I got mad again. Then an idea started jumping up and down in my head. A very sneaky idea. A way to get back at Scarlett. After lunch, I wrote one more letter. This one was to Scarlett.

Hi Scarlett,

I'm sooooooo sorry that I spilled the tea. How clumsy of me. I will be a much better maid next Wednesday, if you give me another chance. I'll bake fancy cookies with frosting. Please say yes.

Love, Lucy

She wrote me back:

Okay.

Little did Scarlett know what I was going to put into those fancy cookies! *Mwa-ha-ha!*

On Tuesday night, I asked my parents for permission to bake cookies. "I want to do it all by myself. They're to share with my friends for a special event."

"Not Scarlett?" Dad asked.

"Actually, yes," I said. "Can I go there tomor-row after school? I want to do something nice."

My mom's eyes got very crinkly on the sides, and she gave me a big hug. "Honey, that is such a sweet plan."

Dad jumped in for a group hug.

It wasn't sweet of me at all, which made my stomach feel terrible. As soon as I got my re-venge on Scarlett, I was going to be nice again. "Okeydokey," I said. "I better get to work."

I used flour, butter, sugar, eggs, vanilla, baking powder, and . . . bugs. Yep. When no one was looking I collected bugs and smashed them up and mixed them in. I only used dead bugs, so the bugs didn't mind. I spread fancy white frosting on the top to hide them. I couldn't wait to serve them at the Craft Cottage.

Mwa-ha-ha!

I did make five cookies without any bugs. I gave one to Leo.

"You are a very smart wolf," I said. "Thank you for teaching me to howl."

He jumped up and licked my cheek and gobbled up his cookie.

Then I gave one to Lily, one to Mom, and one to Dad.

Who got the fifth bugless cookie? Me. Lucy McGee.

Chapter Nineteen

LOOKIE, LOOKIE, COOKIES

After school the next day, Scarlett and I ran to her house. I put on the apron, made the iced tea, and showed off my cookies in the cookie tin I brought.

"Ooh," Scarlett said. "They have frosting. How pretty."

Mwa-ha-ha! Scarlett was going to get what she deserved. A mouthful of bugs. I was going to laugh and laugh and laugh.

Victoria, Mara, and Resa came, and Scarlett started dancing around. They were all wearing their necklaces.

"Welcome again to the Craft Club," Scarlett said. "Come into the cottage for some delicious refreshments. We're going to make matching bracelets today."

Resa smiled at me. "You can sit in my chair, Lucy. I can play the waitress this time."

My throat got a funny lump in it. Resa was nice. She would never make cookies with bugs in them. I felt terrible.

"That's okay," Scarlett said. "Lucy wanted to make us these cookies. Right, Lucy?"

"Um . . . right," I said.

The girls sat down. Scarlett passed around my tin of cookies and each girl took one.

"Thank you, Lucy," Resa said. "These look delicious."

I thought I would be happy, but I wasn't. The kind of happy you get when you do something mean to someone else isn't the good kind of happy.

"Cheers," Scarlett said.

They were about to take a bite.

"Wait," Resa said. "Lucy, you should have a cookie, too." She picked up the tin and held it out to me.

I looked at those cookies. I knew what horrible bits were hiding under that pretty frosting.

"Take a big one," Resa said. Her brown eyes were smiley in a real way. I had to do something. Fast.

I pointed up and screamed, "Spider!"

The girls all dropped their cookies and jumped up. The beads went flying.

Scarlett started screaming and ran out. The other girls followed.

I put all the cookies back into my tin and ran out. "Got to go. Bye."

"Wait, Lucy," Scarlett called out. "Did you kill the spider?"

"Yep. I have to go. Bye."

The last thing I heard was Scarlett's angry voice: "You should leave us those cookies, Lucy McGee!"

Chapter Twenty

STRUMMING AND HUMMING

My feet were on fire. I ran to school and went straight into Ms. Adamson's classroom. The Songwriting Club was still having its meeting. Phillip wasn't the only one in the club anymore. Saki was there with another fifth- grade girl named Natalie and a second-grade boy named Riley. They were sitting in the circle playing their ukes and smiling. The orange uke was sitting on an empty chair.

They all stopped and looked at me.

I looked crazy. I was sweaty. My hair was a mess from running so fast. I was wearing an apron and holding a tin of cookies.

"I keep making bad choices!" I blurted out. "I went to Scarlett's just to get revenge even though I really wanted to come here. Then I came here even though I didn't ask my parents for permission. They think I'm at Scarlett's. Now you probably won't let me in."

"Did you bring us cookies?" Riley asked.

I looked down. "Trust me. You don't want these cookies. It's a long story, but I put bugs in them."

"You what?" Saki laughed.

"I'm sorry I kept changing my mind, Phillip, but this is the club I want to be in. Can I join? Please, please, please. I'm on my knees, knees,

knees." I got on my knees, which actually hurt.

Phillip picked up the orange uke and held it out to me.

Orange *is* the color of happiness.

"Hold on," Ms. Adamson said. "I need to call your parents. If you broke the rules again, they might want you to come straight home."

While Ms. Adamson went to get her cell phone, Phillip looked at us. "We were just brainstorming ideas for today's song."

"Let's write a song about cookies," Riley said. "I like chocolate chip cookies."

"I like peanut butter, too!" Natalie said. "And dulce le leche cookies from Peru! My grandma makes them. Delicious!"

"That's a good start," Phillip said. He strummed his uke and sang.

> *Gimme chocolate chip cookies*
> *and peanut butter, too!*
> *Gimme dulce le leche*
> *cookies from Peru.*

"I like gingersnaps. Oatmeal cookies, too." Riley said.

"Ooh snickerdoodles!" Saki said. "And my grandma is from Honolulu. She makes cookies with coconut. I forget what they're called."

"This is great," Phillip said. He sang:

> *Gimme gingersnaps and oatmeal*
> *and snickerdoodle-doos*
> *and all the coconut cookies*
> *they got in Honolulu!*

104

I jumped in and sang.

> *Just don't give me cookies*
> *with bugs 'cuz it's true,*
> *dead bug bodies are*
> *very hard to chew.*

Everybody laughed.

We were just about to sing the whole song together when Ms. Adamson came back holding out the phone to me.

"Lucy," my dad said. "What's going on?"

"I am having the best time, Dad. Please let me stay!" I said. "I should have called before I left Scarlett's house, but it was an emergency. I'm sorry. My brain was confused. I really want to be in the Songwriting Club! It is very educational. Please say yes."

My dad sighed. "You can stay, but this is your

final warning, Lucy. You have to tell us where you're going to be and stick to it from now on."

"I promise."

"Come right home after the Songwriting Club."

"I will!" I said good-bye and jumped up and down. I could stay!

Ms. Adamson put away her phone, and Phillip taught us how to play the new song.

I wasn't very good at first, but we played the song in slow motion. By the third time, I was a teeny-tiny bit better.

Everybody clapped. It was time to go.

"If we practice over the weekend, we could play this song next week on *The Morning Mix*," Saki said.

"We . . . as in you all and me?" I asked.

"Yep," Phillip said.

Yippie!

"Lucy, would you like to take a uke home to practice?" Ms. Adamson asked.

"Now?" Wow!

Chapter Twenty-One

ME ON TV

Who knew dead bugs could be so inspiring! I played our song with my ukulele on the couch, in bed, at the dinner table, and on the porch. I wanted to play it in the bathtub, but my mom said no. I taught Leo how to play it. I even let Lily hold the uke, but only for one second. She wanted to swing it like a hockey stick, so I took it back.

On Monday the Songwriting Club met at recess, and

we practiced. On Tuesday we got to perform on *The Morning Mix*.

A fifth grader named Pablo was the host. We sang our cookie song.

After we were done singing, Pablo looked into the camera and said, "That was great!" Then he turned to Phillip and asked if he could join the club.

"Sure," Phillip said. "We meet on Wednesdays in the music room."

Pablo smiled into the camera. "I think the Songwriting Club will be performing here again soon! And now, here's the weather."

We tiptoed out of the TV studio and gave each other hugs and high fives.

"We did it! Our first performance!" Phillip said.

Some fourth graders walked by and clapped for us. On the way back to our classrooms more people told us how good we were.

"It's the stars of *The Morning Mix!*" Mrs. Brock said when Phillip and I walked in.

"They just sang one little song," Scarlett said in a mean way.

Resa smiled at us. "That song was hilarious. You guys sounded really good."

"Is Pablo really going to join?" Mara asked. Mara has a thing for Pablo.

Scarlett turned red. "Mrs. Brock," she said. "I don't think it's fair for the Songwriting Club to perform again. Another club should get a turn to be on *The Morning Mix*. I have a club, and we should get a turn."

"I thought it wasn't real TV," I said.

Scarlett made a mean face at me.

"*The Morning Mix* is about school activities, Scarlett," Mrs. Brock said. "The Songwriting Club is for anyone at school who wants to join."

"My club is, too," she said.

"It is not," I said.

She gave me a mean look. "I changed it."

"That's enough," Mrs. Brock said. "It's time for math."

At lunch, Scarlett made invitations and handed them out.

Everyone is invited to my new club next Wednesday called Scarlett's Songwriter Club. We're going to practice a really good song to perform on *The Morning Mix*. Meet me on the playground after school on Wednesday. Free cookies! Pass it on!

Phillip was sitting across from me at the lunch

table. He looked sad. "She's a copycat," he said. "She's going to steal away my people. People like free cookies."

"I left my cookies in Ms. Adamson's room," I said. "We can always serve them."

"Bug cookies?" He gave me a horrified look.

"It was a joke," I said.

He didn't laugh. "You probably want to go to her club."

"No way!" I said. "I promise I will be there. And I will tell everybody to come to your club! It'll be okay, Phillip." I held out my bag of potato chips. "Want one?"

He smiled.

The kind of happy you get when you do something nice for someone else is the best kind of happy.

Chapter Twenty-Two

THE END OF FRIENDS?

Seventy-two cookies! On Wednesday, Scarlett came with a box that had seventy-two fancy cookies in it and more invitations.

Scarlett's Songwriter Club will meet on the playground today! Free cookies!

Phillip looked worried. During math, when Mrs. Brock wasn't looking, he passed Scarlett a note.

I was dying to know what it said.

After math was over, and we were getting our science notebooks out, Scarlett walked by me and dropped the note on my desk.

It said:

We should make one big club. It will be better this way. Meet on the playground. Free cookies! Pass it on.
—Phillip

One big club with Scarlett? Wow. That was a surprise! I passed the note to Resa. She read it and passed it on.

Phillip had a dentist appointment, so I couldn't talk to him at recess or lunch, but

  114

during lunch I told Saki, Natalie, Pablo, and Riley what Phillip wanted.

Phillip came back from the dentist during our last period, but we were too busy to talk. After school, he had to stay with Mrs. Brock a few minutes to get the work he missed, so I grabbed my uke from my cubby and ran out to the playground to make sure that everybody was waiting for him.

Scarlett was on the grassy part of the playground with her cookies. Saki, Riley, and Natalie were there with their ukes. Resa, Victoria, Mara, Pablo, and three other fifth graders were there. Everybody was sitting on the grass except Scarlett, who was jumping up and down and passing cookies around. I joined the circle.

"This is so great!" she said. "I have an amazing song for us to sing on *The Morning Mix*."

  115

Then we all heard a very loud "Hey!" I looked up and saw that the window of Ms. Adamson's room was open and Phillip was looking out.

"You are mean, Lucy McGee!" He yelled it loud enough for the whole world to hear.

My face got hot. I stood up. "What are you talking about?"

"You said you wanted to be in my club," he yelled. "You're a liar!"

"I do. What are you doing in there? You said to meet out here," I said.

"I did not!" he yelled.

"You did, too. You wrote a note this morning and passed it to Scarlett and then she passed it to me."

"I wrote a note saying that I wasn't worried about her club because *you* promised to be in *my* club," he yelled.

What? I stared at Scarlett.

She wouldn't look at me. "Who wants another cookie?" she asked.

"Scarlett!" I said. "Did you copy Phillip's handwriting and make up that note about having one big club?"

"I don't know what you're talking about," Scarlett said. "I didn't pass you any note."

"That's a lie!" I turned and looked up at Ms. Adamson's window. "She tricked me, Phillip!"

"Where's the note?" Scarlett asked. "Prove it."

I didn't have the note.

Scarlett picked up Riley's uke and started strumming even though she didn't know how. "Okay, everybody. Here's how my song goes . . ."

I looked up at poor Phillip all alone in Ms. Adamson's room.

I was so mad and sad. I had to show Phillip that I was on his side. So I did something crazy.

I grabbed
my ukulele and stood under
Ms. Adamson's window and
made up a song on the spot.

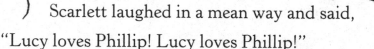

> *You're the kind of friend*
> *that everybody needs.*
> *You can bet I won't forget.*
> *You are the friend for me!*

Scarlett laughed in a mean way and said,
"Lucy loves Phillip! Lucy loves Phillip!"

"Oh, be quiet, Scarlett," I said.
"I'm just singing a song to a
friend. I'm not asking him to
marry me."

Phillip laughed.

Saki stood next to me and

started singing the song, and then Riley and Natalie joined in.

> *You're the kind of friend*
> *that everybody needs.*
> *You can bet I won't forget.*
> *You are the friend for me!*

"We're coming in, Phillip!" I called. I started walking toward the school, singing and playing the uke, and it was like follow the leader. They followed me! Pablo and the other fifth graders joined us. I looked back. Even Resa, Victoria, and Mara were following me! (Well, I think Mara was following Pablo.)

Anyway, we were all singing and dancing our way through the school building toward Ms. Adamson's room. Teachers came out of their rooms to look at us. Mr. Stiles, the custodian, joined in, dancing and singing with his mop.

Phillip was so happy when we all walked in the door and sat down with him in the circle.

Then Scarlett burst in. "This is not fair, Ms. Adamson! Lucy just stole all the people from my songwriting club."

"They were in Phillip's club to begin with," I said.

"Okay," Ms. Adamson said. "Here's the deal. Phillip was the first one to have the idea of a songwriting club. He came to me and asked permission. So he gets to be the leader of the Songwriting Club. Anybody who wants to be in the club can join. Anybody who wants to have their own songwriting club can do that at home."

"That's fine with me," Scarlett said. "I have a very nice Music Cottage. And cookies. Come on,

   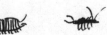

everybody." Scarlett went over to the door and waited.

Nobody moved.

"Sorry, Scarlett," Victoria said. "But this club looks more fun."

"It is fun," Riley said. "And we have our own cookies!"

Riley, Saki, Natalie, Phillip, and Ms. Adamson all laughed at the joke. My tin of bug cookies was still sitting on Ms. Adamson's desk. I had forgotten to take them home.

Scarlett grabbed the tin. "Those were supposed to be for *my* club, Lucy McGee. No takebacks!" She opened my tin.

"Wait!" I said.

She stuffed one of my cookies in her mouth.

Phillip, Saki, Natalie, Riley, and Ms. Adamson gasped.

Scarlett stuffed another cookie in her mouth.

"Scarlett, you might want to take a closer look at what you're eating," I said.

She stopped and looked. Her eyes got big. "Bugs!" she screamed. She ran to the trash can and spit out the cookie. Then she dropped the tin on the floor and ran out the door.

Phillip smiled and picked up the cookies. "I think I'll have one." He lifted a cookie to his mouth, and we all froze. "Just kidding! Let's make up some verses for Lucy's new song."

Phillip started to teach the new people how to strum.

After a few min-utes, Scarlett peeked in the door. She had a puppy face like Leo gets when he wants to play whatever game I'm playing.

"Do you want to join Phillip's club?" Ms. Adamson asked her.

Scarlett nodded and held out her box of cookies. "I'll share my cookies."

It's hard not to feel sorry for somebody who gets a bug in her cookie and loses her friends in one day, even if she kind of deserved it.

"Okay," Phillip said. "As long as you don't try to take over."

"I would never do that!" Scarlett said. She ran in and handed the cookies to Phillip and sat next to Victoria. And she didn't try to take over!

We actually had fun singing and playing to-gether.

Some days are good.
Some days are bad.
This is the best day I ever had.

Hey, that's another rhyme from me, Lucy McGee. See you later!

The End

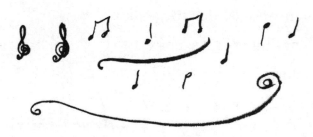

THE SONGWRITING CLUB SONGS

Have fun with the songs
in this book. You can hear
the songs and sing along
by going to the special
Lucy page on my site:
http://www.maryamato.com/
lucy-songs/. You can also find
out more about making up
your own songs and learning
how to play songs on a ukulele,
piano, or guitar.

THE CLEANING SONG

Oh . . . I got a bucket and a brand-new sponge
and I went to a dirty old shed.
I scrubbed the walls and the ceiling and the floor
until my arms were dead.
There were beetles and bugs and ants and slugs
and spiderwebs all droopy.
And hiding in the corner were some little brown bits
where I think a mouse went . . . oopsy!

(Notice that I changed the last
word! If you are singing the song
in the shower at home, you can
sing it however you want. But if
you are singing
the song in school or on
TV or for old people
who faint easily, *"oopsy"*
will be a better choice!)

THE PIGGY SONG

We are the Piggies.
We love our cuddly blanket.
We play so much upon it
we actually should thank it.

Wrap a little piggy
in a blanky . . . so snug!
Come on, little Piggies,
have a Big Pig Hug.

We wag our tails,
and we wiggle them some more.
We say, "Oink oink."
Then we sleep and snore.

Wrap a little piggy
in a blanky . . . so snug!
Come on, little Piggies,
have a Big Pig Hug.

127

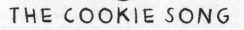

THE COOKIE SONG

Gimme chocolate chip cookies,
and peanut butter, too!
Gimme dulce le leche
cookies from Peru.

Gimme gingersnaps and oatmeal
and snickerdoodle-doos
and all the coconut cookies
they got in Honolulu!

Just don't give me cookies
with bugs 'cuz it's true,
dead bug bodies are
very hard to, very hard to,
very hard to chew.

THE FRIEND SONG

You'd rescue me
if I lost my way.
You'd write a funny
song for me to play.

You'd share your last
potato chips and say,
"You'll be okay. Hey, hey, hey!"

You're the kind of friend
that everybody needs.
You can bet I won't forget.
You are the friend for me.

I make mistakes,
a hundred every day.
I played some tricks
before, I'm sad to say.
But now I want to
make you feel okay.
Okay! Hey, hey, hey!

You're the kind of friend
that everybody needs.
You can bet I won't forget.
You are the friend for me.

SING WITH ME,

LUCY MCGEE

Read a sneak peek from
Lucy's next adventure. . . .

Chapter One

SECRET GROUPS AND MONKEY TROOPS

My friend Phillip Lee walked up to me with a strange look on his face. "Lucy," he whispered. "We need to spy."

We were having indoor recess because of rain, and I was in the Reading Corner of Mrs. Brock's room. Although the book I was reading about animals was good, there is nothing like the word "spy" to grab your attention.

"Who are we spying on?" I asked.

"Scarlett. She's talking about the talent show," Phillip said.

Phillip took my book, and we crept over to the carpet near the cubbies and sat down. We pretended to look at the book, but we were spying. Scarlett and Victoria and Mara were talking on the other side of the cubby wall.

"Ms. Adamson said the talent show is for fourth and fifth graders only, which means it will be really good," Scarlett said. "Little kids would make it babyish."

"So babyish," Victoria said.

"I'm going to write a special song for us," Scarlett went on. "We'll be the best in the whole show."

"Is our group going to be just the three of us singing?" Mara asked. "Or all the fourth and fifth graders in the Songwriting Club?"

"Everybody except Lucy and Phillip," Scarlett said. "Don't tell them."

Phillip and I looked at each other. Scarlett wanted to leave us out?

"I'm going to write my song today," Scarlett whispered. "Let's have a secret group meeting tomorrow at recess to practice."

I couldn't believe it. A secret group without me and Phillip? That hurt.

Just then, Mrs. Brock walked by. "What are you two doing?" she asked us.

"Just reading," I said quickly, looking down at the book.

The girls stopped talking, and Scarlett peeked out.

Phillip pointed to the open page. "Mrs. Brock,

did you know that a group of monkeys is called a troop, and a group of dolphins is called a pod, and a group of lions is called a pride?"

"I did," Mrs. Brock said. "Animal group names are interesting. I'm glad you're enjoying that book."

Our teacher went to her desk, and Phillip and I raced back to the Reading Corner.

"We're all in the Songwriting Club together," I said. "It isn't fair for Scarlett to leave us out. You're the one who started the club, Phillip."

"I know! And you're our best songwriter, Lucy," Phillip said. "The club should sing and play one of your songs at the show."

An idea popped into my head.

"Let's try to write a great song," I said. "We can make it better than Scarlett's song. When everybody hears our song, they'll want to sing and play with us for the show."

Phillip smiled. "That's brilliant! We have to make it a catchy song. Everybody loves a catchy song."

My heart started dancing with excitement. If you are wondering what that feels like, just imagine a troop of tiny monkeys having a party inside you. "Let's do it right now!"

The bell rang.

"Recess is over," Mrs. Brock said. "Clean up and get ready for math!"

Math?

The party was over. It felt like a herd of elephants had stomped in and chased the monkeys away!

MARY AMATO is not just an author of terrific books. She also founded a puppet theater company and is a songwriter and musician who performs regularly in the Washington, D.C., area. Her books for children include The Riot Brothers books, *The Word Eater*, *Guitar Notes*, and *Please Write in This Book*. She lives in Hyattsville, Maryland.